GRANDMA'S GIFT

ERIC VELASQUEZ

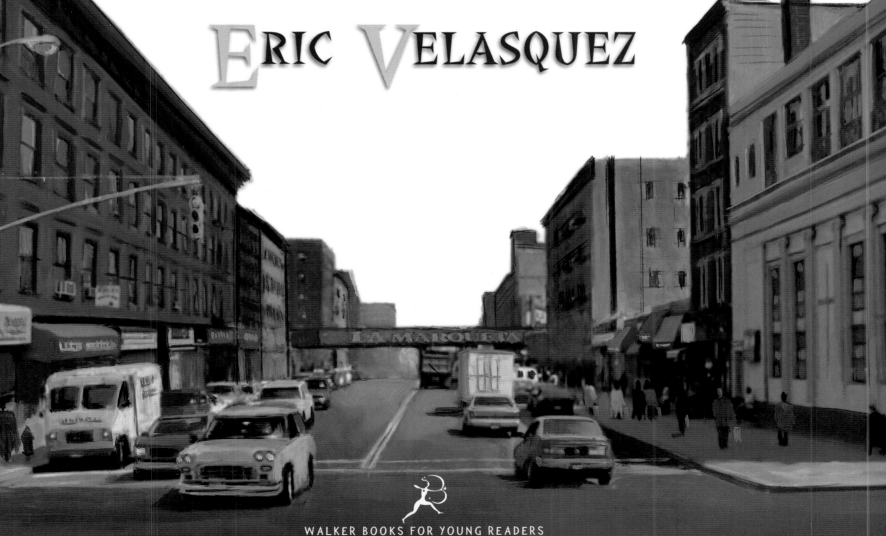

WALKER BOOKS FOR YOUNG READERS
AN IMPRINT OF BLOOMSBURY
NEW YORK   LONDON   NEW DELHI   SYDNEY

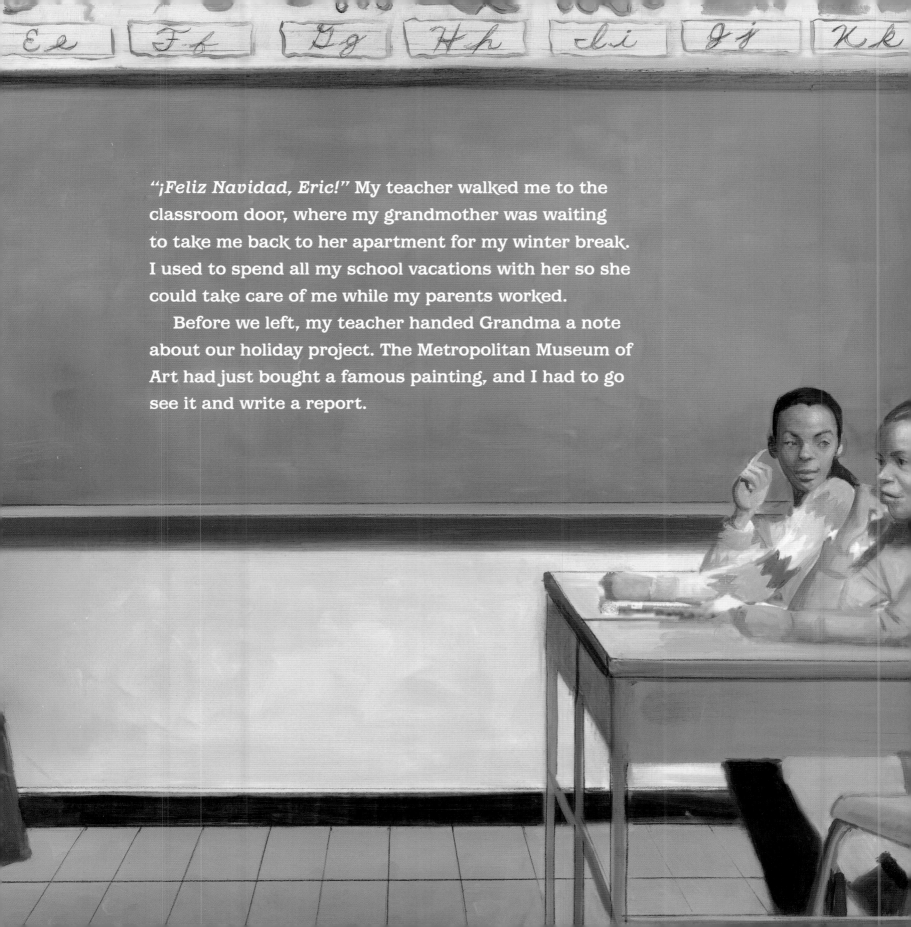

"¡Feliz Navidad, Eric!" My teacher walked me to the classroom door, where my grandmother was waiting to take me back to her apartment for my winter break. I used to spend all my school vacations with her so she could take care of me while my parents worked.

Before we left, my teacher handed Grandma a note about our holiday project. The Metropolitan Museum of Art had just bought a famous painting, and I had to go see it and write a report.

On our way home, Grandma asked me to translate the note because she couldn't read English. I'd translate a lot of things for Grandma—sometimes I felt like I was going to school for two. All the note said was, "Metropolitan Museum of Art, 82nd Street and Fifth Avenue, Second Floor, New Exhibit."

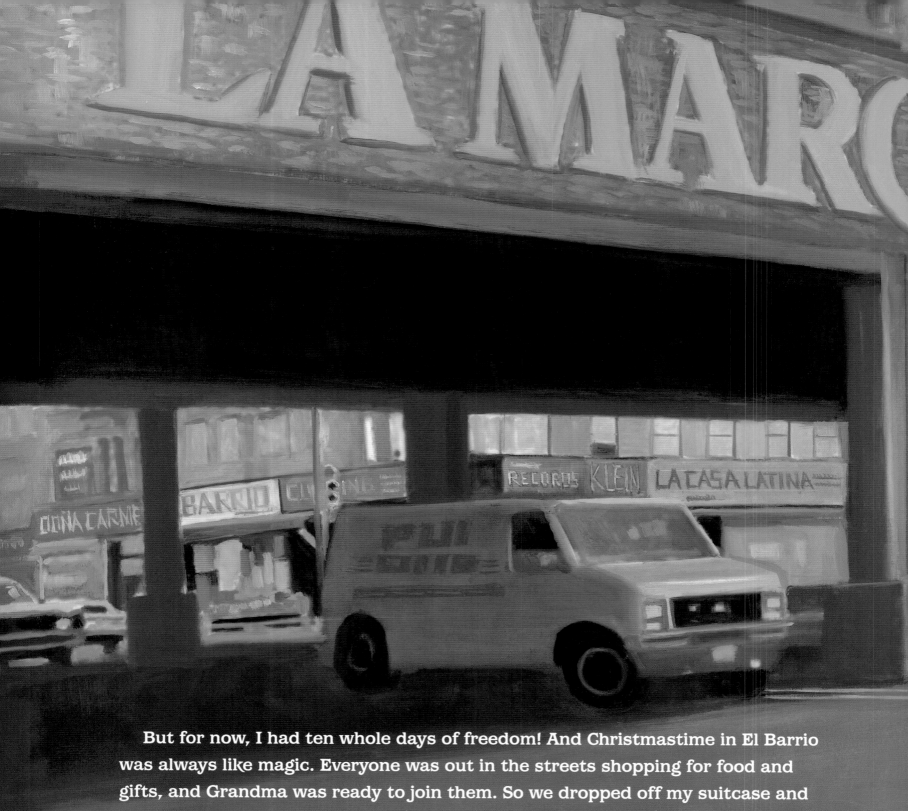

But for now, I had ten whole days of freedom! And Christmastime in El Barrio was always like magic. Everyone was out in the streets shopping for food and gifts, and Grandma was ready to join them. So we dropped off my suitcase and headed straight to La Marqueta (the market)——one of my favorite places.

This special group of shops and stalls sat under the elevated train tracks, and all the stalls rumbled and shook whenever a train passed overhead.

Grandma could find everything she needed there year-round—
fruits, vegetables, fish, meat, clothing, and even her favorite records.
But that day, Grandma was shopping only for the ingredients for
pasteles, the traditional Christmas dish for Puerto Ricans. She
promised that if I helped her make the *pasteles* this year, she would
take me to the museum.

Our first stop was the produce stand to buy the root vegetables.

"*Estoy buscando calabaza, yautía, plátanos verdes, guineos verdes y papas,*" Grandma said to the first vendor. (I'm looking for pumpkins, taro root, green plantains, green bananas, and potatoes.)

"*Pues aquí tenemos los mejores.*" (Well, here are the best.) All the vendors knew that Grandma would buy only the best ingredients for her famous *pasteles*.

When they agreed on the price, Grandma said, "*¡Gracias, y Feliz Navidad!*" (Thank you, and Merry Christmas!)

Our next stop was the butcher stand.

"*¿Cuál pedazo le gusta, Doña Carmen?*" Alberto asked.

(Which piece do you like, Miss Carmen?)

"*Se ve bueno. Dame cuatro libras,*" Grandma said.

(That one is good. Give me four pounds.)

After that, our last stop was
Doña Juanita's bodega for parchment
wrapping paper, banana leaves, string,
and El Barrio's latest gossip.

The worst part of the trip was carrying the heavy shopping bags up five flights of stairs to Grandma's apartment. As soon as she took off her coat, Grandma headed straight to the kitchen and went right to work peeling and grating the root vegetables by hand—never with a blender.

"If you want it to taste traditional, you must make it traditionally," she always said.

When I asked her where she learned to grate so fast, she only answered, "You should have seen my mother grate."

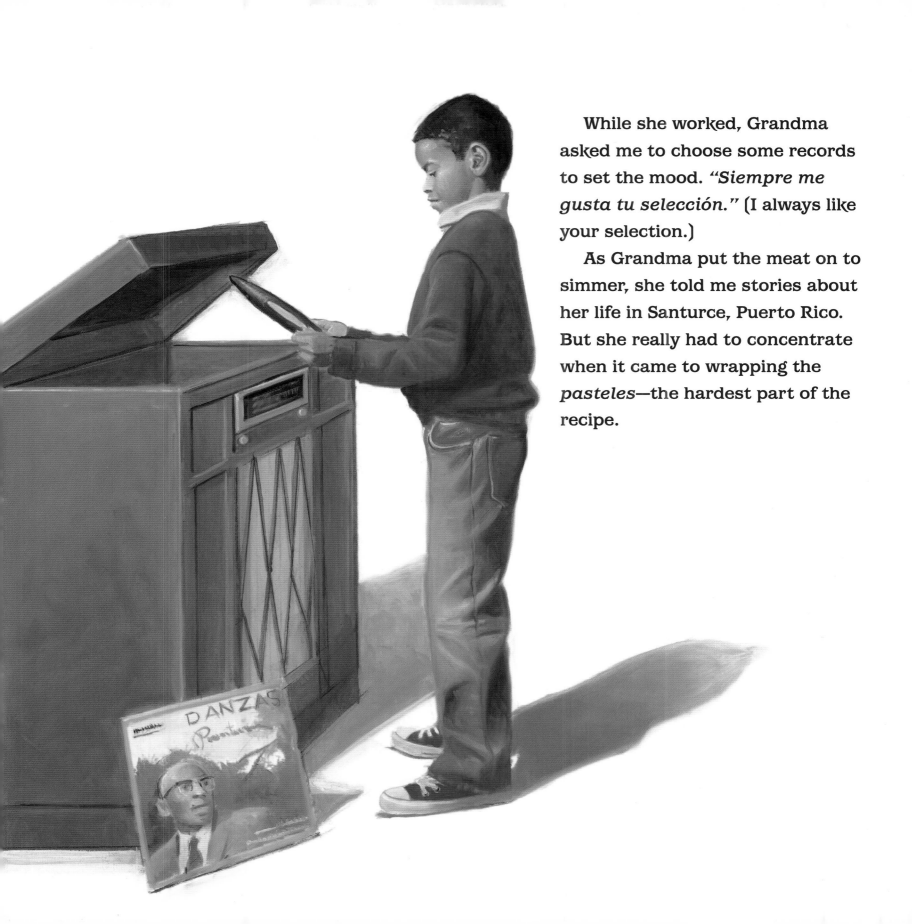

While she worked, Grandma asked me to choose some records to set the mood. *"Siempre me gusta tu selección."* (I always like your selection.)

As Grandma put the meat on to simmer, she told me stories about her life in Santurce, Puerto Rico. But she really had to concentrate when it came to wrapping the *pasteles*—the hardest part of the recipe.

First, Grandma carefully laid out a sheet of parchment paper with a piece of banana leaf on top. Then she poured a little annatto oil on the leaf and added *la masa* (the dough) and *la carne* (the meat)—with a valley scooped out in the middle for *la salsa* (the sauce).

For the finishing touch, she folded everything together to form a perfect rectangle and tied each one with string so it looked like an old-fashioned parcel.

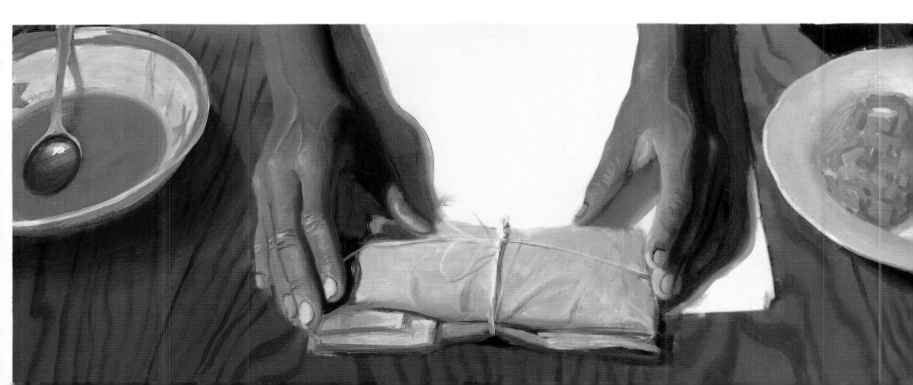

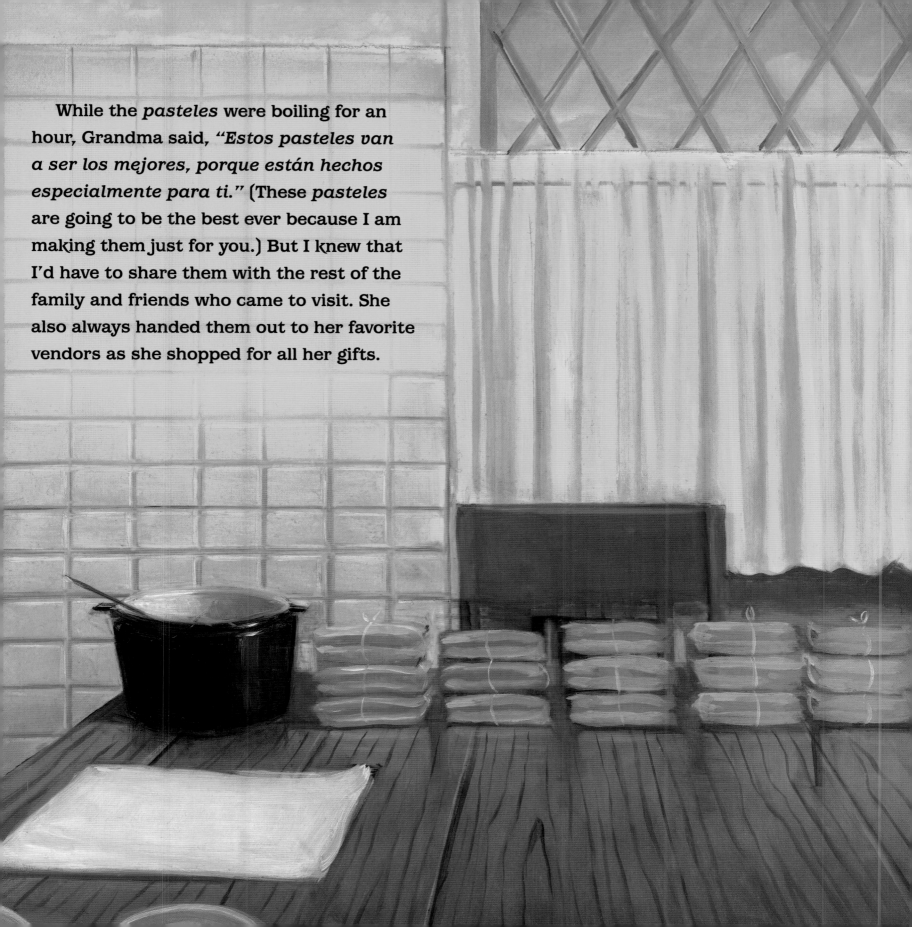

While the *pasteles* were boiling for an hour, Grandma said, *"Estos pasteles van a ser los mejores, porque están hechos especialmente para ti."* (These *pasteles* are going to be the best ever because I am making them just for you.) But I knew that I'd have to share them with the rest of the family and friends who came to visit. She also always handed them out to her favorite vendors as she shopped for all her gifts.

The Tuesday morning before Christmas, Grandma woke up and announced that we were going to the museum—so I could write my report before all the toys I would get for the holiday distracted me.

Grandma never really traveled beyond the twenty blocks that made up El Barrio, where she knew everyone and everyone knew her. I could tell she was nervous, but I couldn't help being excited.

The museum was a short ride down Fifth Avenue, but the neighborhood was completely different. When we got off the bus right in front of the museum, we didn't see anyone from Puerto Rico on the streets and no one was speaking Spanish.

As we walked up the steps and through the doors to the admission booth, I saw Grandma searching the crowd for a familiar face. Then she asked me to read what it said above the booth. I explained that it said to pay what you wish.

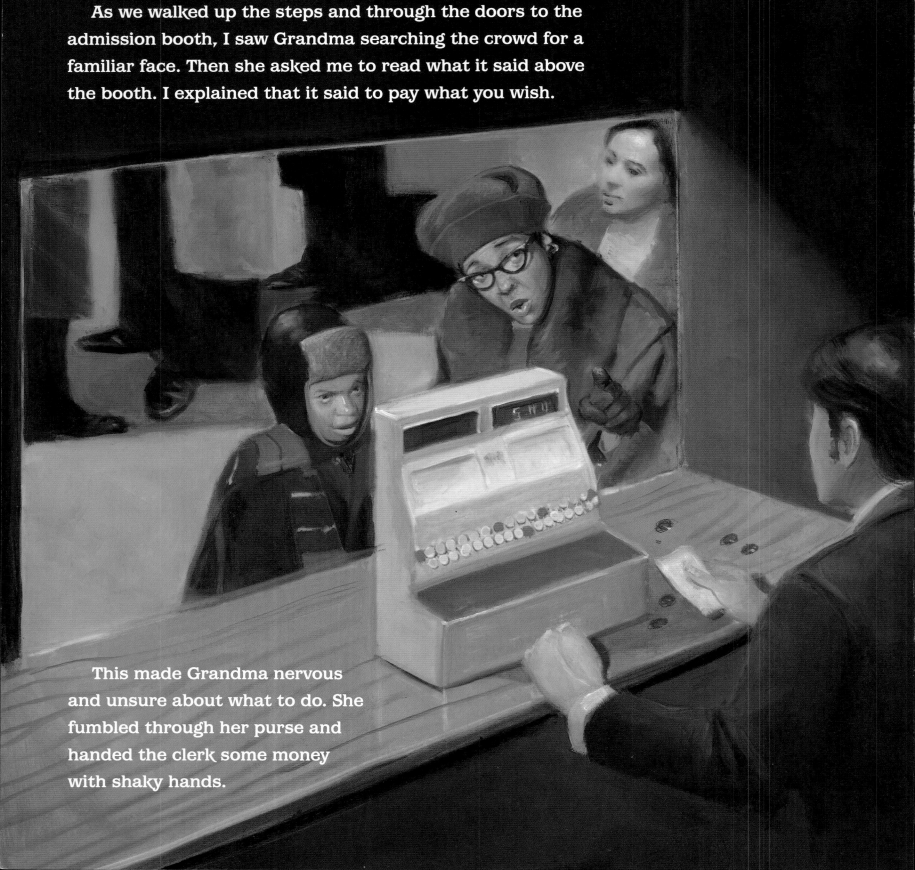

This made Grandma nervous and unsure about what to do. She fumbled through her purse and handed the clerk some money with shaky hands.

Once inside, we went up the large flight of stairs to the gallery on the second floor, as my teacher had directed in her note.

All the paintings there were beautiful. "*¿Qué dice ahí?*" (What does it say there?) Grandma would frequently ask me to translate the caption written next to each painting.

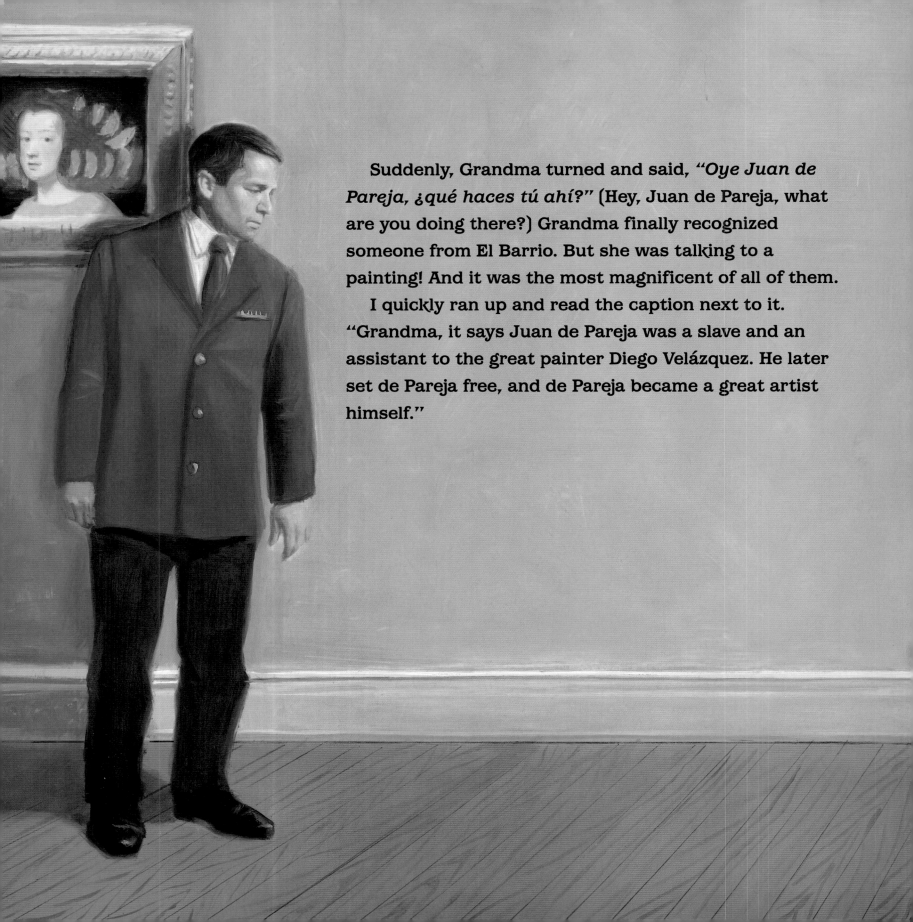

Suddenly, Grandma turned and said, *"Oye Juan de Pareja, ¿qué haces tú ahí?"* (Hey, Juan de Pareja, what are you doing there?) Grandma finally recognized someone from El Barrio. But she was talking to a painting! And it was the most magnificent of all of them.

I quickly ran up and read the caption next to it. "Grandma, it says Juan de Pareja was a slave and an assistant to the great painter Diego Velázquez. He later set de Pareja free, and de Pareja became a great artist himself."

We both stood there, just staring at the amazing painting. The gentleman seemed to be looking back at us. He seemed so real—much like someone we might see walking around El Barrio. I couldn't believe that this was a painting in a museum.

That evening my parents brought *arroz con gandules* and *lechón* (rice with pigeon peas and roast pork) to have with Grandma's delicious *pasteles* for our Christmas Eve dinner. While we ate, Grandma and I told them all about our museum adventure.

Grandma explained that she had learned about Juan
de Pareja when she was growing up in Puerto Rico.
We all told stories and listened to music until midnight,
when Grandma brought out a gift for me.

I ripped off the wrapping paper to find my very own sketchbook and my first set of colored pencils!

As we listened to *"Aguinaldo Puertorriqueño,"* my favorite Christmas carol, I took out my pencils and began to draw my first self-portrait.

AUTHOR'S NOTE

Diego Velázquez's portrait of Juan de Pareja had a profound and lasting effect on me. I grew up in a time when there were very few images of people of African descent in children's books. All of my heroes, sadly, did not look like me.

The portrait of Juan de Pareja showed me for the first time that my people were part of history and not just a casualty of it. He stands so nobly in front of the viewer, as though he wants to tell you his story. The fact that Juan de Pareja was also an accomplished painter himself inspired me to dream of such possibilities for *myself*.

I believe that I am an artist today because of that painting. Yes, it was that inspiring!

After our visit to the museum, my grandma and I went on lots of outings. We visited most of the museums in New York City, as well as the Empire State Building and the World Trade Center. But that day at the museum will always be magical to me.

☙❦

Pasteles (pronounced *pass-TELL-ess*; singular *pastel*) are a traditional dish from Puerto Rico, where the recipe is usually considered a cherished family secret. Making *pasteles* takes a lot of work and a lot of time. (For Grandma's *pasteles* recipe, visit my Web site at www.ericvelasquez.com.) For this reason, most people consider them a special-occasion food—and they are most often made for Christmas celebrations.

Juan de Pareja (1610–1670) spent much of his early life as a slave and as an assistant in the workshop of the painter Diego Velázquez. Velázquez painted de Pareja's portrait in 1650, and it immediately gained him acclaim. Soon after the painting was made, Velázquez gave de Pareja his freedom, though they continued to work together. De Pareja also became an acclaimed painter in his own right. His 1661 work *The Calling of St. Matthew* (sometimes also referred to as *The Vocation of St. Matthew*) is in the Museo Nacional del Prado in Madrid, Spain. Velázquez's *Juan de Pareja* is in the Metropolitan Museum of Art in New York City. It was bought in 1971 for more than $5.5 million, which set a new record for paintings at that time.

"Aguinaldo Puertorriqueño" is a very popular Christmas carol written by the great Puerto Rican composer Rafael Hernández.

For my grandma Carmen; my mother, Carmen Lydia;
and my father, Chu, who now makes the best *pasteles* in El Barrio

(Para mi abuela Carmen, mi madre Carmen Lydia,
y mi padre Chu, que ahora hace los mejores pasteles en El Barrio)

∾

First published in the United States of America in October 2010
by Walker Books for Young Readers, an imprint of Bloomsbury Publishing, Inc.
Paperback edition published in October 2013
www.bloomsbury.com

For information about permission to reproduce selections from this book, write to
Permissions, Walker BFYR, 1385 Broadway, New York, New York 10018
Bloomsbury books may be purchased for business or promotional use. For information on bulk
purchases please contact Macmillan Corporate and Premium Sales Department at specialmarkets@macmillan.com

The paintings in this book (listed in order of their appearance) are based on the following works of fine art
by Diego Rodríguez de Silva y Velázquez at the Metropolitan Museum of Art in New York:
Portrait of a Man, circa 1630, oil on canvas, 27 x 21¾ in (68.6 x 55.2 cm)
María Teresa, Infanta of Spain, 1651–1654, oil on canvas, 13½ x 15¾ in (34.3 x 40 cm)
Juan de Pareja, 1650, oil on canvas, 32 x 27½ in (81.3 x 69.9 cm)

The Library of Congress has cataloged the hardcover edition as follows:
Velasquez, Eric.
Grandma's gift / Eric Velasquez. — 1st U.S. ed.
p.   cm.
Summary: The author describes Christmas at his grandmother's apartment in Spanish Harlem the year she introduced him to the Metropolitan
Museum of Art and Diego Velazquez's portrait of Juan de Pareja, which has had a profound and lasting effect on him.
ISBN 978-0-8027-2082-5 (hardcover) • ISBN 978-0-8027-2083-2 (reinforced)
(1. Grandmothers—Fiction. 2. Christmas—Fiction. 3. Gifts—Fiction. 4. Artists—Fiction. 5. Puerto Ricans—
New York (State)—New York—Fiction. 6. African Americans—Fiction. 7. New York (N.Y.)—Fiction.) I. Title.
PZ7.V4878Gpn 2010   (E)—dc22   2010005326

ISBN 978-0-8027-3536-2 (paperback)

Illustrations rendered in oil on watercolor paper • Typeset in Barcelona ITC Std • Book design by Nicole Gastonguay

Printed in China by Hung Hing Printing (China) Co., Ltd., Shenzhen, Guangdong
1 3 5 7 9 10 8 6 4 2

All papers used by Bloomsbury Publishing, Inc., are natural, recyclable products made from wood grown in well-managed forests.
The manufacturing processes conform to the environmental regulations of the country of origin.